A CHOCOLATE-BOX SUMMER BREEZE

JOSIE RIVIERA

5 STAR READER REVIEWS

Amazon Review by NormaJean:

"Ms. Riviera writes sweet, clean romance stories. This is the fourth book in the Chocolate-Box Series. This story is a little different because Emily and Joe are both older with grown children and grandchildren. I really enjoyed this story of love in the golden years. This book is a quick read and can be read as a stand-alone, but you won't want to miss meeting the rest of the couples in this series."

Amazon Review by Mary G.:

"I enjoyed this book more than I thought I would. It is about two people who are older (my age, actually). They were happy on their own until they got to know each other. Isn't that the way it is supposed to be?"

Amazon Review by Belinda:

"I am in love with this series. A short clean story of two widowers in their 70's who meet and start a friendship that develops over time. Who says you are too old to find love again?"

INTRODUCTION

To keep up on newly released ebooks, paperbacks, Large Print Paperbacks, audiobooks, as well as exclusive sales, sign up for Josie's Newsletter today.

As a thank you, I'll send you a Free PDF ... The Beauty Of ...

Josie's Newsletter

Did you know that according to a Yale University study, people who read books live longer?

This book is dedicated to all my wonderful readers who have supported me every inch of the way.

THANK YOU!

CONTENTS

PRAISE AND AWARDS

USA TODAY bestselling author

#4 Amazon Bestseller Two-Hour Romance Short Reads

#4 Amazon Bestseller Romance Collections and
Anthologies

18 Amazon Bestseller Women's Romance Fiction

CHAPTER 1

At seven o'clock on a Thursday evening, Emily Varon sat alone in a corner booth in Olive's Diner. She swallowed some black coffee, pushed the cup aside and checked her watch.

Joe Vertucci was ten minutes late. Odd, because he was always punctual when he phoned her.

Emily bit her bottom lip, drew back the diner's thick tan-colored curtains, and peered out the window at a sultry California evening. The parking lot was empty except for the few cars that belonged to the customers who were dining inside.

She grabbed her cellphone from her leather handbag and read the last words Joe had texted.

After all these months, I'm looking forward to seeing you in person again, Emily.

Her stomach fluttered as she imagined their reunion. She was looking forward to seeing him too and told him as much. He'd responded with a thumbs-up, which had prompted her to smile. She'd attempted to explain different emojis to him, he didn't always have to use a thumbs-up.

However, he couldn't seem to get the hang of new technology.

Of course, emoji stickers weren't new, and he'd beamed on their video chat when she'd assured that she'd teach him how to use them.

Their only disagreement had taken place when Joe had insisted on paying for their meal. Eventually, she'd conceded and offered to leave the tip.

He'd concluded their conversation with a quip. "That's why I'm crazy about you, Emily. You don't take advantage of me."

Frequently, he'd referred to himself as a blue-collar, working-class guy, and she'd heard a trace of disparagement in his voice, as if he was putting himself down. Although people took pride in referring to themselves in that way, she repeatedly wondered if he genuinely believed in himself.

He should. He was a thoughtful, good-natured man.

Again, her gazed flitted to the window. He could have been delayed by rough weather, or unexpected traffic delays. Hazards on the road occurred in seconds, and driver fatigue often caused serious accidents.

Or, perhaps … Joe wasn't interested in her after all.

She rubbed her cheek with the back of her hand, attempting to pry herself free from the anxious speculations. She hadn't dated in years, and her nerves wavered as if she were a schoolgirl.

This isn't a date, she reminded herself, nor a naïve teenage crush.

She opened the menu and scanned the dinner selections. The special featured grilled chicken, and a baked potato, which suited her nicely. However, the diner's delicious coconut cake would surely ruin her diet.

It was her proper upbringing, she supposed, that kept her focused on the latest fashion trends. Often, though, she pondered if there was a reason to watch her weight anymore. The only people she encountered besides the diners were her son and his family, the weekly grocer, her hair stylist, and Sunday morning churchgoers.

A Moonglow Chocolatiers truck pulled into the lot, and Emily's heart leaped. A man with silver-white hair emerged from the driver's side. Several patrons whispered Emily's name, like the murmurings of a breeze rushing through a forest. Somehow, they knew Joe was here to see Emily.

"I haven't seen Joe in a long time." Oliver, the owner of the diner, stepped over to her booth. He held a steaming pot of coffee.

Emily jumped. She was so focused on Joe's arrival that she hadn't realized Oliver had approached.

"You're eating dinner later than usual." Oliver grinned and gestured toward the window. "Are you waiting for Joe?"

"Yes." Hastily, she jammed her cellphone into her purse. "He's overnighting near here for a couple days."

Oliver refilled her cup. "How did you know Joe was in the area?"

"Why are you asking?" She sat straighter and adjusted her flawlessly creased white slacks. Through all her months at the diner, she'd kept her personal life private. "Sometimes, people need to eat dinner with someone else, rather than all alone."

At the swift, questioning look he shot her, she grimaced. Her response had a breathless, edgy quality. "Sorry."

"No worries, Emily, and you're one hundred percent right. I shouldn't pry." Oliver patted her hand. "I can't help being an old-fashioned Cupid, and I detect a romance is brewing."

"Hardly." She dismissed any further inquiries Oliver poised on his lips with a wave. "Joe and I regularly talk on the phone."

"Ever since you met him here in my diner?"

"Yes," she acknowledged. For an instant, she closed her eyes and relived that stormy February night.

After panicking because she'd never been in a situation like that before—stranded in a diner—her nerves had settled, and she'd enjoyed several hours conversing with Joe. The narratives about his over-the-road travels had made her laugh. It felt good to laugh, especially after she had visited with her son the previous weekend. He, his wife, and her grandchild had been cordial, but their life was hectic and Emily had felt useless and in the way.

She knew they loved her, but they didn't need her.

"May I call you?" Joe had politely inquired that evening, after the road had been cleared and the customers could safely leave the diner.

His request had wrung a reluctant chuckle from Emily, but the sight of his incredible smile had done odd quivery things to her pulse.

She'd agreed and wrote her number on a napkin before handing it to him.

Following an exchange of "safe travels", she'd driven back to her large, empty home in town, and hadn't felt quite so lonely.

"I remember you two got along well." Oliver grabbed a cup and paper placemat from an adjacent table and set them across from Emily. "You never mentioned that your relationship with Joe had blossomed. You eat dinner here nightly."

"Your food is delicious."

"Thanks. I might use your testimonial as advertising." He paused. "However, you're not answering."

"Is this a question or a statement?"

"Both, considering I'm an old-fashioned Cupid," he reminded.

"Joe and I are too timeworn for a romantic relationship."

She tasted the coffee, which was always perfect, then dabbed her lips with a napkin. "Even though I gave him my phone number, I didn't expect him to call me."

"Why not? You're an attractive, classy lady."

She shook her head. She wasn't. She'd continually considered herself plump and the opposite of model-thin, but she wasn't about to introduce a lengthy psychological discussion. Plus, she'd been obsessed with tanning salons, believing a tan made her look younger. However, she'd finally recognized that tanning aged her, and had given that up after she'd met Joe.

One didn't need any more wrinkles at her age.

"Thus," Oliver said, "you've been talking to Joe for—"

"Nearly four months. Joe and I believe in phone calls and occasional video chats," she said.

"There's something about hearing a person's voice. It's more personal."

"Yes, definitely. These days, everyone relies on texting." Emily took another sip of coffee. "Young people stare at their cellphones waiting for bubbles to appear when a phone call accomplishes twice as much in half the time. In addition, there's constantly a risk you'll be misunderstood."

In accord, she and Oliver nodded.

"I'm glad he's here now," Oliver said. "Beneath the flannel shirt and jeans façade, Joe is a romantic guy."

Romantic. The idea brought a funny catch to her chest.

Once, romance had made life worth living.

Now?

She lowered her gaze to concentrate on her cup.

She'd lost all sense of romance after Krandall—her tall, striking husband—had unexpectedly died three years earlier. At the image of his well-heeled demeanor, his poise in the board room, his focus and goal-setting … "I've set my eyes on you, Emily," he'd declared, and the remembrance brought a thickness to her throat. Her moneyed parents had extended not-so-subtle nudges for her to accept his advances so that she could "marry well."

Emily fingered the black-gold and sapphire bracelet, the last piece of jewelry Krandall had bought her before he'd gotten sick.

In fact, he'd purchased many gifts for her, mostly to apologize for his outbursts. He'd been super-critical and continuously chastised her. Sometimes, she believed she was little more than a fixture on his arm that he could show off at high-class fund-raisers.

Glancing up, she realized that Oliver was studying her.

"You're categorizing Joe as a romantic?" she asked him.

"Absolutely. We chatted at length the night he was stranded here, and our conversation was poignant and enlightening."

"Poignant?"

"Guys use fancy words too." He grinned. "From what I gathered, he yearns for a connection with a woman. He was widowed several years ago."

"Companionship … most people are seeking mutual support."

"Joe confided that he longs to feel loved again." Oliver scanned the diner, then set the coffeepot on the table and perched across from her. "Is this a first date? Or a second?"

"Oliver, you're not listening. A widow and widower who are seventy years old don't date."

Although this meeting with Joe was, in every sense of the word, a date. Wasn't it?

No, she repeated to herself.

She fished in her handbag for pink lipstick and a mirrored compact. Ordinarily, she wouldn't fuss as much with her appearance, but the anticipation she'd soon see Joe face to face …

Where is he? the question intruded. It shouldn't take that long to park a truck.

"He's been rummaging for a while." Oliver echoed her thoughts.

Carefully, Emily arranged her silver-blond hair and applied a dab of lipstick. "He keeps track of his hours in a logbook and is doubtlessly making certain the load matches the manifest sheet."

"Manifest sheet?"

"The list of deliveries and shipments." She cast Oliver a sideways smile as he went to the counter to pour two glasses of water.

She'd learned a lot about trucking from her conversations with Joe. What's more, she'd gained an understanding of the man himself. He was frugal, efficient, and fit. He was also sincere, sensible, and because of his job, mechanical.

With an inner sigh, her gaze wandered back to the parking lot.

Tonight was so different compared to the night they'd met. That eventful evening, a severe storm had flattened a tree in front of the diner. Now, four months later, the California rains were nonexistent. Summer bloomed, intense and motionless, the sky a mellow golden hue.

A painter embraced the tints of the sunset, bold tones of orange and crimson. For her, the spectacular evening marked the beginning of another lengthy, desolate season.

Summertime, the potential for light-heartedness and unexpected delight. Days to flaunt straw hats and sundresses, pretty floral blouses, and sandals.

Don't be ridiculous, she scolded herself. The season didn't matter. Not for a grown woman of a particular age.

"What is taking Joe so long?" she blurted, as Oliver returned with two glasses.

7

"Most likely, he's planning something extraordinary for you."

"From the back of his truck?"

Her thoughts drifted to their conversation the previous evening. As was his custom, he'd phoned at six o'clock, and suggested video-chatting.

"I chuckle whenever I consider Oliver and his diner," Joe had said. "The former owners had named the diner Olive, and Oliver kept the name, declaring it had a nice ring to it."

"Even though we've all told him there's a considerable difference between Olive and Oliver."

Joe laughed. "So let's have dinner together at the diner while I'm in town … the place where it all began."

"Where *what* began?" she'd responded.

"Our … our friendship."

Friendship was a safe word. Although, she'd read in a leading scientific journal that men and women weren't capable of being "just friends" because romance bubbled just around the corner.

Her cellphone buzzed. She pulled the phone from her handbag and checked the screen.

"Who is it?" Oliver stood and plucked up the coffee pot.

Her pulse quickened. "Joe is here. He sent me a thumbs-up."

"I know. We saw him get out of his truck, but now I'm staring at him." Oliver pointed to the doorway as Joe entered. "He looks great. Did he lose weight?"

Indeed he had—twenty pounds and counting. She knew he'd been trying because he'd outlined his nutritious diet, reiterating the calorie and fat content.

And indeed he did. Look great, that is.

Joe's handsome, rugged face was clean-shaven. He adjusted his eyeglasses, then shoved a hand in his jeans, his gaze searching the diner. Searching for *her,* Emily realized with a wide grin.

His manner was comfortable, almost boyish. But it was his genuine, inviting smile, a smile that reached all the way to his blue eyes when he spotted Emily, that encouraged her to grin in return.

She stood, flattened her fine, white linen blouse and hailed him. "His route takes him across the state and back," she informed Oliver.

"Sounds like you're proud of him."

Briefly, she savored the moment as she regarded Joe.

"I am," she said truthfully. "We talk for at least an hour until Jeopardy comes on." Her face sobered. She was showing too much excitement. "Oliver, are you taking note of my social life?"

Oliver chuckled and shook his head. "I can hardly manage my own."

"I imagine that Sally Elliot keeps you on your toes?"

Sally was the woman who owned Bloomingfield Candy Shop. She'd been stranded at the diner that same February night along with Emily, Joe, and several others.

"You're imagining correctly." Oliver wiped a hand on his clean white apron. "I see Sally and her daughter, Clarissa, every weekend. Nevertheless, our busy work schedules produce challenges, because I'm here in Evanville and she's in Bloomingfield."

"Challenges you both are apparently overcoming?" Emily teased.

"For love," Oliver replied, "anything is possible."

CHAPTER 2

*E*mily caught a quick breath as Joe hastened to her table. He carried a package wrapped in blue paper, and she silently groaned, hoping it wasn't another baked good. Thus far, the cupcakes and brownies he'd sent to her had been dry and tasteless.

Joe's bright eyes fixated on her. "My lovely Emily." He laid a hand over his heart, confirming he was as elated about their meeting as she. His voice cracked as he placed the package on the table, then took her hands in his—completely disregarding Oliver except for a brief nod. "Thanks for waiting. I'm sorry I'm late."

"Joe, you're only fifteen minutes late. I'm glad you drive slowly and conscientiously." She glanced at her watch. Okay, he was twenty minutes late, but that was because he'd spent a few minutes in the back of his truck.

"By the time I finished my deliveries, then sorted the chocolate—"

"Anything on the road can slow your progress," Oliver broke in. "Did you deliver to Bloomingfield?"

"I did, indeed." Joe winked. "Sally said hello. She and her

daughter will see you later this evening when she gets off work. And tomorrow you're both playing hooky in order to take Clarissa to the aquarium at the new mall in Santa Rosa."

"Exactly the plan." A satisfied grin spread across Oliver's features as he wended around the tables, filling cups of coffee for his customers and stopping to chat.

"How are you?" Joe waited for Emily to sit before settling across from her. She appreciated his gentlemanly traits. He was chivalrous in a traditional manner some people labeled as out-of-date.

Emily didn't. Gallant and respectful behaviors never went out of style.

"I'm fine," she replied. "You?"

He beamed, never taking his gaze from hers. "I couldn't be better."

"You're staring at me as though I have food on my chin."

"I was thinking about how gorgeous you are in person. A phone screen doesn't do you justice. And your hair, it's blonder?"

Self-consciously, she touched her hair. Earlier that morning, she'd asked her stylist to color over the platinum silver. After a half hour of consultation and assurances, Emily had decided the two hours in the salon had been worth it.

"What do you think?" she asked. "It's my natural color, minus the years in between."

He chuckled. "I love it."

"I wanted a change."

"It's a marvelous one … I mean … I liked your previous hair color too."

"It's not that much different."

He studied her. "No, it's just … blonder."

Emily tried not to chuckle at how ridiculous their conversation might sound to anyone who happened to listen.

Judging from the patrons eating and conversing, no one had heard them.

Joe nudged the gift toward her. "I brought something for you."

"Chocolates from Sally's shop?" *With any luck*, she thought. Joe was so intent on creating low-fat goodies he'd forgotten that in the end, taste mattered the most.

"Nope," he said. "I baked these German chocolate mini-muffins in my own kitchen."

She kept her grimace at bay. "Are they healthy?"

"Naturally. I substituted unsweetened applesauce for the vegetable oil. The muffins got jostled during the trip, but I re-wrapped them."

Two weeks earlier, he'd mailed her a batch of chocolate chip muffins, followed by brownies. Each time, he used a thin cord of gold ribbon to create a delicate bow. Although stunning to look at, the baked goods inside didn't prove as delicious as the packaging. The last batch had been too sweet, and Emily had tactfully suggested he use real sugar instead of artificial, which frequently left an aftertaste.

He'd agreed, but the following week, his chocolate-coffee muffins had arrived on her doorstep. Those muffins had tasted odd, and she'd (respectfully, of course), urged him to check the expiration dates on the ingredients.

Sure enough, flour had been the culprit.

She glanced up. Expectantly, he watched her as she examined the package.

"Thank you, Joe. You're becoming a baking expert." She smiled.

A little white lie never hurt anyone.

She nudged aside the fake potted lilac plant Oliver always placed on every table, unwrapped the package, and peeped inside. Immediately, she inhaled the aroma of rich, dark chocolate.

"I bought a new bag of flour," Joe said.

She extended a brilliant smile. "Thus you baked two perfect muffins."

Hopefully.

"Maybe not perfect, but I figured that after dinner we'll try them for dessert."

"Joe, you always persevere."

"All I can do is try."

He was sincere and put his whole being into everything.

The knowledge caused her to smile. "Oliver's special dessert tonight is coconut cake," she said.

"My muffins have fewer calories than cake." Absently, Joe perused the menu, then grasped her hands. "Is there anything in the world more captivating than you?" he asked softly.

She moved back. "What brought on that compliment?"

"You. Just seeing your lovely face and new hair style."

"New hair *color*," she corrected. "My style is the same." With a laughing sigh, she leaned her head against the green vinyl seat. "There are countless subjects more captivating than me."

"You're not a subject. You're my Emily."

She concentrated on his words. Nonetheless, she drew her hands away and clasped them properly on her lap. They were friends, she repeated to herself, and she wasn't about to get cozy in a public diner. She'd grown accustomed to living life alone, although, through Joe's direct and indirect hints, she intuitively knew he craved more from their relationship.

Joe frowned at her response. There was that directness about him she admired, the way he wore his sentiments on his sleeve. Her late, by-the-book husband had controlled his emotions.

Krandall had been a generous provider, fixating on his net worth and savvy with his fortune, believing the money from his investment business liberated them.

Joe remained silent, evidently waiting for her to say more. When she didn't, he said, "We've established dessert. What is your choice for dinner?"

"I've decided on the grilled chicken special and a bowl of Oliver's homemade vegetable soup."

"Low calorie and hearty, but please choose the most expensive meal on the menu." He held out his palms in a generous gesture. "Remember, dinner is my treat."

"The grilled chicken is the most expensive entrée tonight."

He laughed. "Then I'll have the same, because this is a celebratory evening."

After they'd placed their order with an efficient teenage waitress, Emily leaned in. "Do you eat all your meals in diners, Joe?"

"Usually." Yet again, he grasped her hands. "What about you?"

"I never eat out anywhere but here, and only for dinner. I prepare my other meals at home."

"We should dine together more often. When I'm driving, all I can think about is phoning you from my hotel room. You're the highlight of my hours and I love hearing your voice."

The heartfelt attentiveness in his gaze and the enthusiasm in his tone made Emily feel warm and cherished.

"I feel the same," she said. In fact, his calls had become a lifeline, and she looked forward to telling someone about her day. "Although I wish you'd cut back your working hours— for your sake."

"I can't, Emily. I'm paying off my daughter's college tuition loan because she recently lost her job. As a single mother, Lydia is struggling. She applied at the bank for a debt consolidation and seeks employment every day."

You're struggling financially too, Emily thought, but she didn't share her contemplation with him.

The fact that he was compelled to work an exhausting job in order to pay his daughter's bills brought a sadness, an infuriation, to Emily's chest. By now, Joe should be ready to retire.

Managing his route and the truck's contents while staying on schedule was arduous for a younger man, and ever more so for someone Joe's age. Yet, he managed it all while maintaining a courteous demeanor with his suppliers and customers. Even when describing his workdays he never complained, and she innately knew he wouldn't welcome her observations or sympathy.

Emily blew out a breath. "Your actions are admirable. However, your daughter is a grown woman."

"Wouldn't you do the same for your son? From what you've mentioned, he's doing well financially, but if he wasn't—"

"Naturally," she agreed. "But I wish you would relax more."

"Relaxing isn't a word in my vocabulary." Joe downed his water, then fidgeted. "So Emily, where do we go from here?"

"We? Why? Where are we going?"

For the first time, she questioned if there was another purpose for their arranged meeting that Joe was easing into. Since this was a special and upbeat reunion, she followed his lead. Perhaps she'd shift their discussion to small talk, rather than student loans and debts. At cocktail parties in the past, she'd been a pro at engaging people in light conversations.

"It's a figure of speech." Joe cleared his throat and scratched his chin. "I have the next few days off."

"Good. You deserve it."

"How about you?"

"I don't work."

He scanned her face. "I mean, what do you have planned for the weekend?"

"Nothing."

Oliver wandered to the juke-box, and the jingle of coins dropping in the slot followed as he selected a song, throwing a grin at Emily over his shoulder.

Several seconds later, Frank Sinatra's voice crooned the first few measures of *You Make Me Feel So Young,* an upbeat romantic swing jazz piece.

She grinned at Oliver and awarded a wave. There was something about being in a familiar place—with an attractive man who was obviously interested in her sitting across the table—that brought an excitement she hadn't envisioned. Add the music, and the night was magical.

"Are you a Frank Sinatra enthusiast?" Joe inquired.

"I love his music, particularly *Come Fly With Me.*"

"I'm a Beatles fan."

"Rock?" She scoffed. "All the music sounds the same —rebellious."

"Not the Beatles. Their music is fresh and innovative. How about country songs?"

"No, but I adore musicals," Emily replied. "Especially *Cats,* by Andrew Lloyd Webber."

"I've never seen a live musical, nor listened to any."

"You've never visited New York city, or strolled on Broadway?"

"Nope." He sat on the edge of his seat. "What's the musical about? A cat?"

"Several cats, and my favorite song is 'Memory'." With a soft murmur, she called up the lyrics … "being alone in the moonlight with remembrances of the past."

"Is there a storyline?"

"Of course. The old cat, Grizabella, is mourning her

youth." Emily tipped her head to the side. "Sometimes the older you get, the more it seems like you've disappeared."

Sometimes, oftentimes, she'd felt that way with her son and his family.

"What's your favorite song?" she asked. "Besides anything by The Beatles."

"Give me any tunes by Journey."

"You're going on a journey?"

"Journey is the band's name, Emily."

She offered an abashed smile. "I'm joking."

"I know." He shifted but didn't grin. "Are you spending the Fourth of July with friends?"

She automatically tensed at the question. Any social life since she became a widow was nonexistent. Her core of socialite friends had avoided calling, and Emily learned that several wives considered her a threat because she was single.

To keep active, she'd tried a sip and paint class before concluding she wasn't good at sipping wine or painting. Hence, she'd given up on a night life, or a day life, or any social life, for that matter.

"No plans," she replied.

Joe kept his features reserved, although the affection in his deep-blue eyes betrayed him. "Will you see your son?"

"He and his wife and my grandson are taking a hiking trip to the mountains."

"They didn't invite you?"

"Not in so many words, but I suppose the invitation was there." She kept her voice a monotone. "I'll call him. That is, if he has cell phone service where they are camping. Oftentimes he doesn't pick up. However, I always leave a message."

Joe extended a half-smile. "I do the same."

"Our adult children and their families lead hectic lives."

"Yes."

Emily focused on the ceiling. "Anyway, I've never slept in

17

a tent before and informed my son that I'm certainly not starting at my age."

"So you prefer creature comforts?"

"Totally. You?"

"Delicious food, a pleasant home, and a delightful woman by my side is my vision of paradise," Joe said. "I could probably climb into a sleeping bag ... however, climbing out is a different matter entirely."

"Because of the zipper?"

"Because I'm seventy." He smirked. "It's not easy for me to get up."

His upbeat banter was so infectious that she grabbed his hand before she could stop herself. "Not exactly a simple task for me, either."

"Unless we're both planning to become Olympic athletes in our seventies, sleeping in bags on the ground probably isn't a satisfactory plan. You're physically fit, though, Emily. I presume you work out."

There was no mistaking the admiration on his features.

Her face flushed. The two-mile walk on the treadmill every morning was tiring, but obviously worth it.

She drew back but didn't release her gaze.

"My daughter and her little girl won't be around either." Joe picked up his coffee cup and smiled at her over the rim. "What I'm trying to ask is ... are you interested in riding to Cambria with me? I'm scheduled to pick up another chocolate delivery near there, but not until Monday. Therefore, my days in between are clear, plus I'm paid for the vacation."

"And you choose to spend those days with me?"

"Absolutely."

"You mean ... ride with you to Cambria ... in your delivery truck?"

"Sure, and we can enjoy the long weekend together. Cambria is a little seaside town. I've visited a number of times because there's a major chocolate distribution center close by. Tourist attractions in Cambria include a castle and a boardwalk, and we can watch the sunsets on Moonstone Beach."

Emily attempted to tamp down her excitement, although her senses reeled. "Where is Cambria?" she hedged.

"About five hours away."

"I'm not sure—"

"No pressure." Joe set down his cup and grasped her hands again. "No expectations. Just two friends taking pleasure in one another's company."

She eyed the Moonglow Chocolatiers truck in the parking lot. "Is there enough room for me?"

"I'm driving a box truck, Emily. There's plenty of space."

"I'm not accustomed to packing lightly."

"Bring whatever is best for a beach trip, especially if it fits into a duffel bag."

She frowned. She couldn't recall if she even owned a duffel bag, but she owned a set of white designer suitcases.

"Fair warning," Joe said. "If I keep any clothes and items in the back, they tend to smell like chocolate."

"Tend?"

"They do. They will."

With a quiet giggle, she assured, "Chocolate is my favorite."

"Me too, or I wouldn't have lasted two decades transporting it across the state."

She pressed her lips together, still debating. "Is there a downside of riding in a truck?"

"Well, dust always lands in the passenger seat."

"Can anything go wrong on the road?"

"Plenty." He caressed her fingers with his thumb. "A punctured tire, a cracked windshield—"

Halfheartedly, she stifled a grin. "Joe, are you trying to talk me into going? If so, you're hardly succeeding."

"Because I saved the best for last." He sat straighter. "My truck has something no other can boast. Besides having you along for the ride, of course."

"Which is?"

"A year ago, I installed an eight-track cassette tape player in the dashboard."

"The proprietor agreed?"

"I leased the truck for five years, and now I own it."

"I commend your entrepreneurial spirit, but where did you find cassettes?"

"Several big-box stores, vintage record shops, and online. It's a niche industry, but many people prefer tapes."

"Therefore, there is no CD player in your truck?"

He quirked a white eyebrow. "What are those?"

"CD's are—" She caught his smirk and joined in. "At any rate, eight-track cassettes are antiques. Like us."

"We're not antiques, Emily. We have an exciting life ahead of us and an entire world to experience."

She shrugged. "Maybe." She wondered exactly where that world was located … sometimes. At other times, she was content in her quiet, daily routine.

Wasn't she?

Of course.

Moreover, repetition was excellent for aiding memory, and her routine was invariably the same. She drove the short distance to the diner for dinner, conversed with the other customers and Oliver, and returned to her comfortable brick house in the center of the small adjacent city.

Rinse and repeat, her conscience chided, noting that her days had become repetitive and dreary. Was Joe's invitation an opportunity for adventure?

"What are the accommodations in Cambria?" she asked. "Are there hotels?"

"There are numerous motels and hotels and quaint bed-and-breakfast spots. At last count, Cambria's population was around six thousand."

"You described a seaside town." Emily envisioned starfish, tumbling waves, and a smart pier harboring million-dollar yachts.

"Cambria is near the Pacific Ocean," Joe continued. "The community boasts an abundance of sea life, including otters and seals. We can book a boat excursion if you'd like. I did once when I was there … by myself." He paused. "We can swim, although parts of the coast are rocky."

Emily's head came up at the swimming reference. "Decades ago, I was a member of my college's swim team."

"What was your best stroke?"

"The backstroke." She met his gaze. "Were you on the swim team in college?"

"I didn't attend college, but I know how to swim. To support my family, I took the first job offered as soon as I graduated from high school. My father had died when I was young, and my mother cleaned houses for a living. We constantly struggled to make ends meet."

When she didn't respond, Joe granted a broad, disarming grin. "May I confess something?"

"Why not?"

"I rented a tiny, quaint cottage by the sea. It's not as fancy as the deluxe resorts where you vacationed when Krandall was alive." He hesitated. "I know you summered in Europe and wintered in the Bahamas."

She shook her head. "Contrary to what you might presume about me—"

"You prefer the finer things in life."

"Admittedly, but Cambria sounds enchanting."

21

Joe blinked. His eyes rounded. "My tiny cottage will suffice?"

"Nicely." She bit back a smile at his enthusiastic tone. "However, if you've already rented the cottage, then you assumed I'd agree to your invitation?"

"I wasn't certain." He squeezed her hands. "Nonetheless, I was hopeful."

She turned to the window. Night had descended, the golden colors of afternoon had dimmed to twilight, then blackness.

And there was one more subject to resolve.

"Joe, without sounding prudish ..." She subjected him to a delicate raise of her eyebrows. "We both were married, but my mother instilled Victorian values in me that I still ascribe to."

"Excellent." He grinned. "Your mother must have known my mother."

When he continued to grin, Emily reiterated with utmost honesty. "Consequently, I won't share a bedroom with you."

"I respect you too much to ask otherwise. The cottage I rented has two bedrooms, and I'll sleep in the smaller of the two."

CHAPTER 3

*W*as this beach trip a wise idea?

The following morning, Emily pondered the question while she finished packing. She'd selected casual, comfortable clothes. After all, it was a spur-of-the-moment invitation. For the drive, she opted for a black and white jersey knit sundress, black leather sandals, a thin silver bracelet, and a cardigan sweater to drape over her shoulders.

When had she last gone on a vacation, or anywhere at all since Krandall had died, except to visit her son and his family?

Pausing to rest on the tufted sofa in her cozy sitting room, Emily set the duffel bag on a table and drew a knitted blanket over her lap. Because of the air conditioning, she was often cold.

She leaned her head back. Too excited to sleep the previous evening, she'd risen when stars still flickered in the sky. She hardly ever slept well anymore, waking frequently.

After their dinner at the diner, Joe had phoned when she'd returned to her house, describing in enthusiastic detail the places in Cambria she might be interested in—the charming boutiques lining the boardwalk and an artifacts gallery displaying art painted by local California artists. She envisioned a Nantucket-style cottage, a coastal retreat with lattice greenery growing over the roof. A sunny, gleaming oasis decorated with cane chairs and needlepoint pillows.

A thumbs-up text from Joe brought her to her feet. She stifled the kick in her pulse as his truck rounded the street corner.

A minute later, she was partway across the living room when the doorbell rang. Although she was overjoyed to see him, she was determined to stay poised and attempted to tamp down her enthusiasm as she opened the door.

He stood on her front steps with his hands dug in the pockets of his khaki shorts, wearing a smile that revealed white teeth. His strong pride showed in his rough-hewn features, and the firm mouth that had tenderly kissed her goodnight.

He wore sunglasses, quickly pointing out they were prescription when she complimented him on his appearance.

He held her hands in his, then slanted his head. "How much stuff are you bringing?"

"Stuff?

"Clothes … stuff."

"This and that. Somehow, I managed to fit most of my toiletries into a duffel bag."

"Somehow? Almost?" He peered around. "I don't see a duffel bag, but I do see two large white suitcases."

"My duffel bag is in the sitting room."

"Sitting room?" He shoved up his glasses. "What's that?"

"A place where you … sit. I needed something slightly bigger and couldn't fit all my clothes into one little bag."

"A duffel bag expands."

"Not enough," she countered. Because she'd added another one-piece swimsuit, a cover-up, two more

24

sundresses, nightclothes, a bold pearl necklace, white cotton slacks, and a couple flowery-print blouses. In addition, her makeup and night clothes took up more space than she'd anticipated, which had necessitated the second suitcase.

Joe rubbed his temples. "I'll store your suitcases in the back. Be ready to smell like chocolate when you open them in the morning."

"You warned me already, and I'm prepared." She hung her hands on her hips, opting for a more logical approach. "What woman can fit all her weekend outfits into a duffel bag, anyway?"

"Certainly not anyone as fashionable as you." He placed his arm lightly on her shoulders. "I phoned my daughter. Did you speak with your son?"

"He seemed pleased I had plans for the holiday." *Immensely, overly pleased.*

With a twinge of heartache, Emily had detected her son's relief. Definitely, she was joyful because he had a devoted wife and an adorable son, but oftentimes she felt abandoned.

"Excellent." Joe brought a hand to his forehead and peered toward the hallway. "Are you ready?"

"Whenever you are." She retrieved her duffel bag, secured the windows and snatched her purse, and house keys.

Joe lifted her suitcases and feigned an amplified groan. "Imagine if we traveled for a week. What would you pack then?"

"Enough for at least four suitcases." At his incredulous stare, she quickly inserted, "Just kidding."

As they walked to his truck, he paused to regard her. "I still can't believe I persuaded a fine, wonderful woman like you to come along with me."

"It was the eight-track cassette player," she reminded with a laugh.

He opened the passenger door, then waited as she

climbed in and buckled her seat belt. "Thank you for agreeing to ride with me, Emily. This trip means more than you can imagine."

"Me too," she said quietly.

He was a thoughtful man with a tender heart, and she hardly was able to contain her happiness that she'd met him.

He started the ignition and eased onto the street, then the interstate, while Emily fiddled with the radio stations. When the disc jockey's voice introduced the next song as country/western, a man in an SUV pulled up next to them at the stoplight. His SUV blasted the same station.

"My cassettes are in the glove compartment." Joe had evidently noticed Emily's pained expression as Willie Nelson blared from their twin speakers. A woman, apparently, was always on Willie Nelson's mind.

Emily sifted through the row of cassettes—ranging from The Eagles to an assortment of Beatles collections—and her hand stilled. "Frank Sinatra's Greatest Hits? The soundtrack from *My Fair Lady*?"

"I couldn't find the musical you mentioned … the one about dogs."

"Cats," she corrected. "And I thought you didn't care for—"

"This morning, I patronized an oldies store in town."

"You were searching for music for me?"

"Only for you," he said affectionately.

She was special to him, and the knowledge filled her with delight.

The miles passed rapidly, and Joe remarked on the numerous tourist attractions. Traffic moved at a crawl when they hit construction sites, and he braked slowly and gently. Whenever they picked up speed, acceleration was seldom quick.

"We're in Bloomingfield," Joe announced when they drove

along the main street of a charming town. He angled his steering wheel toward the curb. "This is where Sally Elliot owns her candy shop."

"Don't stop," Emily said. "Sally isn't working today because she and Oliver and her daughter are visiting an aquarium."

"Oh, right." Joe stared out the front window and carefully merged into traffic. "Her sister, Julie, owns The Pasta Junction, a fine Italian restaurant here in town, and she makes her own pasta. Her eatery doesn't open until dinnertime, though. Have you frequented either place?"

"I don't travel much farther than the diner," Emily answered with a broken laugh. She shook off her defeatism and said graciously, "But Oliver's food is tasty."

"His meals are the best in the state," Joe agreed. "We'll stop in Bloomingfield some other time, alright?"

"Alright."

He glanced at her. "Is that a promise?"

"Indeed." Emily nodded and stretched out her legs. Her limbs felt weightless, and her expectations were positive.

Some other time. A promise of a next time.

"I've never ridden in a truck before," she confessed. "I'm up so high."

"There's a first for everything, and the view is better."

"Is driving difficult? The ride is a bit rough, and I noticed you swing wide on your turns."

"Yep, and I take ramps and curves unhurriedly."

For the next half hour, they covered an expansive stretch of highway while serenaded by Frank Sinatra's soothing voice singing, "That's Life." Up ahead, a billboard advertised a fast-food restaurant at an upcoming exit.

"Are we stopping for lunch?" Emily asked. "I'm content eating at a drive-through."

"I packed sandwiches," Joe replied. "Or rather, the deli prepared them. There are several roadside picnic areas."

"I haven't picnicked since … forever."

"The spot where I'm headed is on a riverfront."

"Krandall preferred to dine at the country club," Emily mused.

"Nothing against a country club, although I've never even entered one. I prefer to eat outdoors. Food tastes better, particularly a classic turkey sub with roasted red peppers, which I requested especially for you."

She clutched her fingers together. "How did you know some of my favorite foods?"

"Easy." He chuckled at her reaction. "I phoned Oliver. I ordered the same sub for myself, except I requested mine garnished with green peppers instead of red."

When they broke for lunch, she heartily agreed that food tasted better alfresco, further declaring she was becoming a nature lover. To her surprised pleasure, she wasn't immune to the ambiance of an unassuming meal and devoured an amazingly marvelous lunch. As she reached for a cold bottle of water from the sack of drinks and sandwiches, she marveled at the backdrop of their location—the grove of redwood trees, the rushing river, and the scenic, towering mountains.

They disputed whether green or red peppers were tastier, and she did fun things—simple things—such as sitting by the river and skipping rocks.

"Find the smoothest, flattest rock," Joe instructed, demonstrating that a simple flick of the wrist produced the best bounce. "Also, face the water."

"Where else would I face?" She laughed out loud, relishing the friendly competition as she thrust rapidly and the rock flew airborne.

"Next time, I'll teach you how to spin rocks," he said. "You're certainly a pro."

"My newfound skill," she jested, "is skipping rocks."

"You beat me on every throw."

She shoved the hair off her forehead, her lips twitching with laughter as she embraced the finest, most relaxing day she'd ever experienced.

But of course she was with Joe, and as she'd previously determined during their numerous conversations, he had the ability to change ordinary events in life into memorable ones. No fancy meals for him. Just plain old-fashioned fun that didn't rely on a high-priced atmosphere or over-the-top chef creations.

Afterwards, Emily lounged against the truck while Joe filled the tank with gas. She relished the soothing breeze against her face and the brilliant glow of the afternoon sun, grateful for the straw hat she'd worn to protect her complexion.

In a few short hours, they exited the highway. The day had flown by, and soon they arrived at the cottage. Emily rushed across the stone walkway, taking in the appeal of the classic Cape Cod style—the weathered cedar shingles and white wooden shutters.

And then she stopped.

The cottage looked neglected, as if it hadn't been updated in decades.

"The website stated that the cottage had a run of owners, but the reviews were pretty good," Joe said. "Plus, the rental rate was reasonable."

Pretty good. Reasonable. Emily made a quiet groan in her throat. Half of the dilapidated wrap-around deck faced the shimmering Pacific ocean, and two rusty pink bicycles sat propped against an abandoned rose trellis.

"I haven't ridden a bike since I was a teenager," she

murmured, sidestepping the fact that the bicycles screamed for a major repair, as did the rest of the property.

"Neither have I." Joe gestured to a younger woman who stood on the sandy beach and stared at them. With his arm draped around Emily, he steered her toward the doorway and tipped her chin up. "I bet our neighbor thinks I should kiss you before we enter our weekend escape."

Emily tucked her hands at her sides. "I bet she's not thinking any such thing. She doesn't even know us."

He lowered his head. "Let's show her what two happy people look like … two people on top of the world."

Emily bit back a helpless smile as their lips touched. "Make it quick," she murmured.

"I can't kiss you quick when you're laughing."

"I'm laughing because you are."

As their breaths merged, he extended a friendly wave to their neighbor.

THE MUSTY, dry odor of the cottage's interior hit Emily first.

"This place was advertised as sparkling clean and boasting divine beds," Joe muttered.

"Nothing that an airing can't solve," Emily chirped. "We'll open the doors and windows."

They stepped on creaky, white-washed wooden floors and came upon the larger of the two bedrooms. A red and white buffalo checked quilt covered the single bed. An ancient air-conditioning unit blocked most of the cracked window, and slivers of light shone through. Outside, rolling sand dunes, and tall grass swayed in a wind gust.

"If I owned a cottage in a splendid location like this," Emily said, "I would remodel the bedroom, install central air-conditioning, and let the sunlight in. The view of the ocean is spectacular." She ran her fingers over the dusty oak veneer chest and studied a watercolor depicting a fisherman's boat set against a backdrop of jagged cliffs. Emblazoned in blue letters on the boat's stern was *Summer Breeze.*

"Sometimes, owners name their boat after a pleasant memory," Joe remarked.

"Summer Breeze brings to mind hope and joy. It's easy to forget any concerns with the promise of summer to cheer you." Emily balanced on her toes to examine the initials etched in the right-hand corner. "K. S. Who do you suppose that is?"

"There was a Keaton Smith art gallery in town a few months ago when I was here," Joe replied. "Let's include the gallery on our itinerary."

"I like itineraries." Emily offered a smile, then reluctantly returned her attention to the bedroom, particularly the cobwebs. Her smile faded as she pondered how long it had been since the walls had absorbed a fresh coat of paint, or the four rooms had been filled with the aroma of a Sunday pot roast.

"When you stare at the floor," Joe said, "you make me think the cottage is inadequate."

Quickly, she shook her head. "No, no, not at all. It's lovely …really. Only, I'd anticipated something more modern." Belatedly registering his wounded expression, she focused on a point over his shoulder, regretful for allowing her expectations to prompt her to blurt her reservations aloud.

Several seconds of unpromising silence followed.

She stiffened, expecting a verbal set-down. When Joe didn't respond, she encouraged, "Please talk to me. I'm sorry."

"What would you like me to say?"

"To begin with, you can chastise me about my comment."

"I'd never chastise you."

"Okay, but you can tell me that I was rude and ungracious."

"I won't do that, either." He sighed. "This is a cottage built in the 1920s, Emily. You can't expect modern. I told you it was quaint."

"I realize you tried to find the best place on a budget." She drew a long breath. "Are you upset by my remark?"

"I'm not sure."

"I don't understand."

"When it comes to you, my thoughts haven't been clear since we met. In addition, my insecurity grows heavier every second we're together." He kept his stare downcast, which prompted Emily to smile.

She rattled him because he was attracted to her.

"I'm thrilled to hear that," she declared.

Joe didn't appear nearly as thrilled. He rubbed the back of his neck, sat on the edge of the bed, and invited her to sit beside him. "We should come to a clearer understanding of what is happening between us, and, more importantly, how we should continue."

"Joe, we just arrived. This conversation is too serious."

He steepled his hands. "Shall I speak first, or you?"

She flinched. He'd ignored her statement.

"Go ahead," she relented.

"Fifty percent of the time I shake myself, a reminder that I'm really here with you and this isn't all a dream," he said. "You're too attractive and elegant to devote your days to a guy like me."

"Don't put yourself down. I respect you a great deal."

"We're not having this conversation because I'm fishing for compliments, Emily."

She fingered the silver bracelet on her wrist. "And the other fifty percent?" she prodded.

"Despite how well you may perceive me and my lifestyle,

I'm a galaxy away from being inexperienced. The perfectionism I strove for in my youth, the same perfectionism I believe you still want, disappeared for me many years ago. We're both seventy and should acknowledge our differences. I'm the opposite of a wealthy millionaire. I earn an hourly wage and will never receive a six-figure, end-of-year bonus." The grin had long since vanished from his features. "This isn't a senior prom, and I'm not speculating about whether I'll kiss you, because I already have, and—with your permission—will do so again."

Her cheeks heated. He was frank about expressing his feelings. She liked that.

Politely, she folded her hands. "Are you finished?"

"Should I be?"

"Can't you understand that I'm proud of you and what you've accomplished?"

"I own a delivery truck, Emily, and my house is a quarter of the size of yours."

Their earlier excitement was rapidly disintegrating, and an imperceptible strain slowly descended on the tiny bedroom.

"Those things aren't important to me," she replied.

He tapped his fingers on his knee and didn't look convinced.

She inhaled and smiled. "Well then, everything is settled."

"What's settled?"

"You have my permission."

"For what?"

She peered at the doorway. "It's been nearly a half hour since you kissed me and …"

Realization dawned on his face.

Smiling, he cupped her chin and silenced her next words with his lips. As further proof she was sincere, she flung her arms around his neck and returned his kiss.

Several minutes later, they walked hand in hand through the narrow hallway to inspect the galley kitchen, which was painted a dark cobalt blue and boasted glass cupboard doors.

She scanned the chipped Formica countertop. "Where's the coffee machine and pods?"

"There is a coffee pot on the stove." He indicated a stainless steel percolator, then stepped to the white refrigerator and peeked inside. "I also arranged a grocery delivery for necessities."

Sure enough, a quart of milk, a dozen eggs, a loaf of bread, butter, bottled water, and ground coffee perched on the top two shelves.

"You planned everything." She darted a glance at the shabby surroundings, forcibly reminding herself that this was a beach cottage, not a five-star resort. "Where is the bathroom?"

"It must be through here." As he freed a jammed door, his voice went quiet. Water leaked from the sink's faucet, and the mirror reflected tarnish. Although only one person at a time could fit in the cramped space, the tiles gleamed and fresh white towels hung on the towel bars.

She peered inside. "There's no shower stall."

Joe strode to the living room and grabbed a brochure off the coffee table. "I read about an outdoor shower, but I assumed it was to rinse off the sand after a day at the beach." He swung wide a saloon-style door in the kitchen which led outside.

"Hmm."

"Hmm?" she asked.

"I guess the shower is truly outdoors." He hesitated before facing her. "I assume that's okay … because … because you're a nature-lover, right?"

CHAPTER 4

*N*ature, Emily soon realized the following morning when she stepped into the outdoor shower, presented a challenge. And clearly she wasn't a nature-lover after all.

Spiders and creepy-crawlies naturally gravitated to a damp area. In addition to the leaves and sand piled in the corner, clouds rolled in while she was soaking wet and the wind picked up, leaving her shivering and taking the fastest shower of her life.

And then there was the bigger problem.

In addition to the compactness of the space, she was *exposed.*

Not to mention that she had to hang her rosy-red sundress and clean undergarments on the door and hoped they didn't fall into the dirt while she quickly scrubbed herself. Thankfully, the warm water, plus the fragrant euca-lyptus spearmint soap she'd brought from home lifted her spirits.

She didn't bother with make-up except for a pastel pink lipstick, foundation, and mascara. She had secured her neatly coiffed hair with a shower cap beforehand so it didn't get wet, and later swept back the ends with a thin, glossy-red headband.

Despite the obstacles, she was determined to impress Joe.

Why did she care about impressing him? she challenged herself. They were two friends sharing a weekend. Romance wasn't part of the equation. Furthermore, there was no attraction between them.

Hah, her conscience chided, and she thrust it aside. Oftentimes, her conscience was an annoyance.

A half hour later, fully dressed and made-up, she slipped on easy, closed-toe shoes and entered the kitchen.

The front door and windows were wide open, and the weather promised a silvery-blue sky and comfortable temperatures. Emily caught a whiff of a salty sea breeze and the echoes of percussive waves hitting rhythmically against the shore.

Joe stood near the stove, brewing coffee and popping bread into the toaster, and his efficient movements made her smile. The attractiveness of his robust physique, his purple polo shirt tucked into navy shorts, hastened her breathing. Feeling suddenly shy, she shoved her hands into her pockets and wished him a cheerful good morning.

"Good morning, beautiful." He met her smile, and her heartbeat doubled at the affection in his gaze. "Red becomes you."

She braced her fingers on the counter and took a slow breath. *Friends, friends, friends*, she reminded herself.

"How was your shower?" he asked.

"Quite an adventure." *Talk about an understatement*. "A stunning sanctuary isn't the first description that comes to mind."

"The second?"

"Um, no. Perhaps airy?"

36

"Therefore, the experience was …"

"Harrowing. And my clothes smell like a chocolate factory."

"I warned you." He grinned. "I encountered a large spider."

"That's all?" She laughed, then feigned disappointment. "You were lucky."

"Why? What did you see?"

"The better question is … what *didn't* I see?"

He barked with laughter. "I rose before dawn and showered early."

"I didn't hear you."

"You were fast asleep. Did you rest well?"

"Surprisingly, yes. I opened my window and the sound of the ocean waves lulled me to sleep. Usually it takes me a long time to fall asleep."

"Me too, but not last night. It must be those divine beds." She giggled her assent as he reached into the cupboard for mugs and poured two cups of coffee. She inhaled the deep, rich aroma.

"You take your coffee black, right?" he inquired.

She nodded and relished the first sip. Of course he'd remembered her preference.

Standing, she spread butter on their toast, and they worked companionably, bantering while they set their dishes in the sink after a light breakfast.

"No dishwasher," he murmured. "Sorry."

"I can certainly wash and dry a few dishes. There's nothing to apologize for." She glanced his way and her pulse quickened. Her feelings for him multiplied the more hours they spent together.

"Let's venture into town and stock up on more food supplies," Joe suggested. "I want to try a new recipe while we're here."

"Another brownie that promotes weight loss?" Emily teased.

He draped a dishcloth over his shoulder and perched his hip at the edge of the table. "Lydia emailed me a recipe for peanut butter bars. She insists they're delicious." He pulled out his cellphone and scrolled.

Emily eyed the tiny stove, and oven, then peeked over his shoulder. "All my favorite ingredients. Butter, peanut butter, and chocolate."

He frowned. "Hardly low-calorie."

"Excellent news." Emily placed the last of the clean plates in the cupboard. "A modest amount of fat isn't necessarily bad, as long as you balance the foods with a nourishing meal plan."

He didn't appear convinced but tucked his cellphone into his pocket. "This afternoon we can visit William Randolph Hearst's castle. I reserved two tickets for a tour of the grand rooms."

CHAPTER 5

A few hours later, as the tour guide detailed the history of the magnificent Hearst Castle, Joe scanned the gardens, then concentrated on Emily. With her hair pulled back by a red headband and a hint of pink lipstick on her full lips, she presented a stunning vision. Her complexion was clear, and her heavenly blue eyes were framed by black lashes and elegant eyebrows.

"Can you believe the castle took all those years to finish?" Her demeanor was upbeat, and her gaze shone with excitement as she pointed out the architecture surrounding the opulent pool.

Joe nodded. "Right."

"From 1919 to 1947! And building on the mountaintop in order to capture the breathtaking views was brilliant. I am in awe of Mr. Hearst's vision."

Again, Joe nodded.

She squinted and slipped on her sunglasses. "Hence, you agree?"

"Yep."

"Uh, huh. Did you hear what I said?"

"Of course."

She hung her hands on her hips. "Tell me, then, word for word."

"You began with … we're on a mountaintop." He continually lost his train of thought as he gazed at the curves of her figure, her stunning smile, and the sun shining on her face.

"Therefore, you weren't listening. First, I remarked on the views because they are awe-inspiring." She drew in a breath. "I wonder what the rooms that were not included on our tour look like."

"You do?"

"Yes." She paused, and he sensed an uncertainty in her voice. With any luck, she was exploring a dignified way to suggest another road trip with him.

"You'd like to see more of the castle?" he encouraged. "With me?"

"Am I that transparent?" Studiously, she observed the rose bushes and avoided his gaze. "You must realize you're the ideal—"

"Companion?" He drew her nearer and chuckled, the scent of her spearmint fragrance uplifting. Steadying himself, he pondered why she had such an insane effect on him. "You're my ideal companion too."

She hesitated and pulled at the neckline of her dress. "Joe?"

Whenever she uttered his name, her delicate, pure voice had a dreamlike quality that stirred his senses.

"Hmm?"

"I'm glad we met."

"Me too." He held her close. "I believe fate has a hand in these things—how people meet, when they meet. Sometimes events take place that are beyond our control."

Slightly, her lips parted. "Fate is from the Latin word, fatum, which means 'that which has been spoken.'"

"Did you study Latin in college?"

She rested her head on his shoulder and grinned. "I read a lot, but I learned that from Webster's Dictionary."

THE REMAINDER of the day was a blur of shared hugs and a peaceful walk on the beach. Later, a stroll through town revealed that the Keaton Smith Art Gallery had shuttered a few months earlier. However, they appreciated the sense of originality in the flourishing community that especially beckoned to Emily. She stopped often and browsed—particularly at the stalls where local jewelers created white polished necklaces, rings, and matching bracelets, and crafters wove bright-colored quilts.

She purchased a nautical souvenir for her son's home, plus a bag of caramels for her grandchild, and Joe did the same.

When an antique dealer invited them inside his shop, Emily murmured that his pieces seemed ideally suited to the cottage's ambiance.

"You mean because they're old?" Joe jested.

"Nothing can be as old as that cottage," she solemnly returned.

Simultaneously, they both laughed.

He hugged her then, right in the middle of the shop. He couldn't get enough of her, which was a unique experience for him. Since his wife had died a decade before, he'd found little claim in socializing because no woman appealed to him. Sure, his friends arranged double-dates, but Joe had made up his mind. He wasn't interested in anyone or anything except his daughter, his grandchild, and his work. Any dreams before his beloved wife's death had been lost.

That is until now.

Emily fit effortlessly in the curve of his arm. She was

appealing, curious, and captivated him with stories about her experiences traveling around the world—Europe and Asia and Africa—places he'd never envisioned outside of magazines and television. In her enthusiastic style she'd encouraged him to imagine new possibilities again.

He'd also been impressed by her understanding of technology when she'd adeptly showed him where to find the emojis on his phone. That had resulted in a half hour of experimentation as he'd texted her pink hearts, red hearts, dazzling hearts, and an array of golden stars that had prompted her to giggle until tears streamed down her cheeks.

Sometimes she was stubborn, other times she charmed him with her smile. She was refined and elegant, never showy, topped with so much love bottled up that she mesmerized him.

"All my life I've lived for my son," she said.

"Live for yourself, not others," Joe replied. "Although it's entirely understandable when it comes to our children. They are an important part of who we are."

Emily's eyes had glistened with tears. "There are instances when my son is too preoccupied to spend time with me and I miss the noise and clatter of a crowded household. I remember when I believed the outside world was fraught with peril, and my mission was to protect him."

"You describe memories I also hold close to my heart," Joe admitted. "I miss those years too."

He was living proof of that emptiness. It was the main reason why he preferred to be on the road—to avoid going home to a desolate, lonely house.

Although he and Emily were the same age, he was a million times more world-weary, because he had grown up in a poor neighborhood, whereas her life had been one of affluence. Nonetheless, something about her relaxed him, and that was novel.

However, she avoided any discussions about their future, explaining she didn't wish to ruin their hours together with talks about anything other than the present. Besides, they were too old for any of "that foolishness."

The foolishness of love?

Or was she ashamed of him, his modest background and line of work, and too considerate to vocalize her feelings? He was suitable for a fun, light-hearted weekend, but beyond that ... nothing.

He'd always been a plain, unassuming guy, accustomed to simplicity. At eighteen, he had taken the first job that had come along and was grateful. He'd noticed Emily's barely disguised disapproval when he'd mentioned assisting his daughter financially and couldn't understand why it seemed to upset her. At his stage, he was pleased to help his family while they were down on their luck. In addition, he'd managed to tuck away a fair amount of savings.

ON SUNDAY, Joe spent the afternoon assembling ingredients for the recipe his daughter had sent. Emily came and stood beside him in the kitchen and assisted. As a team, they creamed butter, spooned in the peanut butter, and measured the oatmeal.

After the peanut butter bars finished baking, they assembled a tray and two mugs of herbal green tea and headed into the living room. The only TV displayed a makeshift antenna, and they caught tidbits of black and white Andy Griffith Show reruns, which suited them nicely. The everyday activity of passing time—relaxing and watching TV with a special woman—was something he hadn't enjoyed in years.

As Emily placed the half-eaten tray of cookies on the

coffee table, he spoke with a grin. "I decided I prefer regular butter over the low-fat stuff."

"Hurray and don't forget extra chocolate." She stood to brew more tea. As he observed her walking gracefully to the kitchen, he admired her effortless, natural style and the understated sophistication in which she carried herself.

At his insistence, she'd dressed up for their Sunday together. She'd strung a large pearl necklace around her elegant throat, and her deep-blue sundress matched the color of her vivid eyes. With her shiny hair pushed back, her face radiated a sun-kissed glow. After getting ready, they'd found a white-steepled church in town and attended services.

After the service, he'd caressed her cheek and kissed her.

"Tomorrow is our last day," she said, and he detected the conclusiveness in her tone. Or perhaps he imagined it.

"Unfortunately, yes," he replied, his voice shaky. "But we have several hours together while we pick up the delivery, and the ride back home."

He envisioned her attending various social functions when she was married to Krandall—charity balls and Broadway musicals in New York City, and couldn't imagine how he'd forgotten that he'd never be a part of those scenes. He wouldn't escort her to extravagant events because he couldn't afford them. Furthermore, his awkwardness would embarrass her.

In that instant, he understood that not having her in his life was going to be hard, but there was no other choice. Emily deserved better than anything he could offer.

Vacantly, he focused on the paneled wall in the living room as a hollowness filled his chest.

"What are you thinking?" she asked, returning with two steaming mugs.

"Nothing." He shifted. *Nothing he would share with her.*

He offered his best imitation of a smile. "Shall I bake the

next cookie batch using spray butter and artificial sugar?" He suspected that she didn't care for his low-calorie baked goods. She'd never told him, not in so many words, but oftentimes a person conveyed more by what they didn't say, rather than by what they did say.

"No! Please!" Emily sputtered, almost dropping the mugs before setting them on the table.

"I can save several hundred calories—"

"At the expense of taste."

"I've lost weight since I lowered my calorie intake," he loftily responded. "However, this is our vacation, so I'll just sit on the couch and eat more cookies." He gave her a side-long smirk, snatched a cookie from the tray, and took a bite. "Although the middle is undercooked."

Emily nestled closer, and he shared his cookie with her. "Blame it on the tiniest oven in the universe, not your daughter's recipe."

"Are you saying … never blame the cook?"

She laughed and lifted her lips to his. She tasted of chocolate and sweetness and all that he'd missed for so many years. "Never, ever blame the cook."

"Emily, you're the best thing that has happened to me in a long time," he whispered. "Always remember that."

If she wondered why he'd uttered that last part, she gave no indication. Instead, the bonus for his admission was a dainty brush of her fingers against his chin, and a kiss that stole his breath away.

SEVERAL HOURS LATER, they rode in his truck to Moonglow beach and strolled the planked wooden walkway of the boardwalk. Along the way, they searched for moonstones. Yes, there were really moonstones, he assured Emily, and many people made jewelry with them—such as the necklaces and rings and bracelets they'd admired in town. As they found shiny black pebbles and polished sea glass, they often rested on the benches lining the pathway. Joggers ran past, riders on bicycles flew by at a brisk clip, and a couple stopped to converse—describing the playful seals they'd spotted earlier in the day.

As Joe and Emily continued, an easy summer breeze ruffled Emily's hair, and the tang of the ocean filled his nostrils. Fingers entwined, they admired the rock-strewn cliffs and jaw-dropping coastline.

"We didn't have time to take the boat excursion," he said. "Or to swim."

"Maybe next time."

He turned to gaze at the ocean, his heart heavy, knowing there would be no next time.

One last night together.

He wanted all that they were sharing—tomorrow, the day after that, and the day after that. He longed to paint the town red... would she know that old expression? He suspected she would.

He yearned to embrace life and celebrate every hour with her, because time went by too quickly.

She snuggled against him and he squeezed his eyes shut for a moment. Nearby, people threw red, white, and blue confetti in the air, waved American flags, and cheered.

He soaked in the ambiance of the enchanting pint-size community, its gentler pace, and the way the sun scattered bits of golden sequins on the Pacific Ocean. Fireworks marked the July Fourth celebration, and patriotic music blasted from a loudspeaker in the distance.

A flood of affection, of contentment, radiated through him.

He loved their little cottage. Unquestionably it showed

maturity, but the weather-beaten shingles proved it had lived successfully through another season, despite its age.

Much like him. Much like Emily.

He loved this ageless place that hinted at a kinder lifestyle from a date long forgotten.

And then he realized what he'd known in his heart all along.

He was in love with Emily Varon.

CHAPTER 6

*S*unrise came quicker than expected, and Emily snuggled under the buffalo-checked red and white quilt longer than she'd planned. A sea wind whistled through the cracks of the window as she reluctantly opened her eyes.

They were leaving.

Quickly she showered and then packed, appreciative of the coffee and toast Joe had placed on the oak chest in her bedroom. When she tried to swallow, the coffee tasted bitter in her constricted throat, and the toast was dry and flavor-less. A disturbing awareness hit her, setting in motion sadness and confusion. She didn't want to return to her private and solitary existence.

Making a concerted effort to maintain her composure, she pondered why this trip with Joe had come to mean so much.

However, she couldn't let him know, choosing not to appear needy. Especially when she suspected that her son and his family considered her clingy and desperate.

She finished arranging the last of her toiletries in the duffel bag and stepped to the doorway. The Moonglow

Chocolatiers truck idled, exhaust coiling densely from the tailpipe into the sultry morning air.

"Good morning, lovely." Joe adjusted the emerald-green silk scarf she'd tied carelessly around her throat. "Are you ready? I brewed an extra thermos of coffee for the ride, and I included leftover peanut butter bars to nibble on before we stop for lunch."

Emily bobbed her head, but her legs refused to move.

"There's rain in the forecast. I'll need to drive slower and keep my lights on." He peered at the gray clouds on the horizon, then hoisted her suitcases.

"Okay. I'm in no hurry." Emily went into the kitchen and slowly picked up the coffee pot, disposing of the coffee grounds and washing the mugs and plates they had used. She held Joe's mug against her heart, tracing the rim with her finger before she placed it back in the cupboard.

With a muffled sigh, she glanced around. Much as the cottage was in disrepair, she would truly miss the place.

After they collected the cases of chocolate at the delivery center outside of town, the rains started. Joe kept the radio volume low and made no mention of playing any cassette tapes. He increased his following distance and kept the truck at a deliberate, safe speed.

After an hour, he pulled into a rest area, and Emily grabbed the thermos and poured them coffee. They stood under a tree, and a car sped past, splashing water against the truck.

Hazardous weather. Rain. Construction. Joe was under a considerable amount of strain, regularly driving under challenging conditions, and this had been his occupation for countless years.

They stopped several more times for gas and food, and the mood remained solemn.

They made it through Bloomingfield an hour later than it

had taken to cover the same distance in sunny weather. Soon, they would be back in her hometown.

As they covered the last stretch, Emily sat straighter and gathered her courage. She'd never declared her feelings openly, certainly not to a man she'd known for mere months.

Nonetheless, the time had come.

She couldn't envision a life without Joe, couldn't accept the agonizing awareness of resorting to repeated phone and Skype calls with him again.

Despite her jittery stomach, she dismissed her reservations and single-mindedly focused on one objective. She didn't care anymore about sounding needy. In truth, she *was* needy when it came to continuing their relationship. And she would tell him, employing her 'small talk' finesse.

"Joe?" she began.

"Hmm?" He kept his gaze forward, the wipers beating a recurring back-and-forth flap against the windshield.

"I'd like a more permanent courtship."

So much for finesse.

He blinked. For a split-second, he took his gaze off the road and regarded her.

"How? I constantly work, Emily."

"Perhaps you can drive less." She took a quick breath. "Or, preferably, not at all."

"I need to continue working."

She pushed on, crossing and uncrossing her legs. "Move to my town, so we can be together more often."

"You're talking marriage?"

"Well—"

"In summary, I'd have no income and would rely on your money to support me?"

"I didn't say that."

"I noticed you didn't ask to move in with me. I assume you're ashamed of my house, although you've never seen it."

His shoulders curved forward as he concentrated on the road. "Let's face it, Emily, you're ashamed of *me* because I'm a common truck driver."

"You're misconstruing all my words."

"Am I? What would my daughter reckon, and my fellow drivers, if they learned I was with you? They'd suspect I was after your wealth."

"You assume this is about money, and you're worried about your self-esteem?" Letting out a shocked gasp, Emily sat back. "It's about a full-time relationship rather than a part-time one. I deserve better than that."

"You deserve better than *me*," Joe countered. "Someone who fits into your world."

She flinched, and her stomach hardened. As they passed Olive's Diner, she stayed silent. When they arrived at her house, Joe parked the truck and came around to open the door for her.

"Thanks for coming with me," he said briefly, and leaned forward.

In case he wanted to kiss her, she held up her palm to ward him off.

He grimaced, grabbed her suitcases and duffel bag, and carried them into the living room.

"Thanks, Joe. Goodbye. Safe travels." Her chest hitched. She couldn't say more.

His grimace remained. "Goodbye, Emily." He stumbled back a few steps, then spun. Without another word, he got into his truck and drove away.

CHAPTER 7

*S*even days went by. Then fourteen.

Despite her efforts to occupy herself, Emily pined for Joe, missing him desperately. He'd sent a brief text saying he was driving to another part of the state and would be gone for a while.

And then, nothing.

Naturally, she was too proud to phone him, and awaited a call that never came. Obsessively, she checked her phone and waited.

The weekend they'd shared had begun like a fairy-tale. Oftentimes, she imagined another scenario, a happier ending. If only their relationship had turned out differently.

Yes, she loved him, and believed he cared for her.

But now it was over.

On a typical Thursday evening a week later, she sat at a corner booth in Olive's Diner, staring out the front window at the sunset. Fresh pink and tangerine orange colors ignited the sky. The month of July was coming to a close, and the days had been reduced to a smudge of summer. She'd gone into town more often, holding on to the breeze as she chatted with people she passed. It felt wonderful not to disconnect from strangers anymore.

She'd even enrolled in a painting class again, surprising herself when she discovered that she did better when she put forth more effort. Her earlier lack of talent had grown from mental obstacles, and she'd been hesitant to try anything new since Krandall's death for fear of failure.

Failure was a matter of one's experience, she supposed. The fear of risking her heart and subsequently losing it, had almost broken her. That is, until she'd relaxed her tight muscles, taken a fortifying breath, and stepped into the art studio again. Her first attempt had produced a watercolor of a fishing boat, which she'd proudly hung on her sitting room wall. On the stern, she'd penned, 'Summer Breeze' in scripted calligraphy. In addition, she'd filled her home with vases of pink and yellow seaside daisies, a display of cheerfulness she seldom felt.

Oliver stepped to her table, bringing her musings to the present.

"The air-conditioning broke," he said.

"I noticed it's warm in here tonight, but I don't care for air-conditioning, anyway."

"Have you seen Joe lately?"

She swallowed hard. "No." They'd been over this every day since she and Joe had parted.

"Are you ordering tonight's special?" He grabbed a pencil from behind his ear and tugged an order pad from his apron. "I'm serving lasagna."

"Excellent. I expect the pasta is loaded with extra ricotta cheese and heaps of calories."

"Guaranteed." He tapped his pencil on the edge of the table and peered at his watch. "Look, Emily. I wanted to surprise you and probably should have told you earlier, but—"

"Lasagna isn't a surprise, Oliver." She gazed at him with frustration. "You serve lasagna on alternate Thursdays." She glanced out the window and her head jerked back as a familiar Moonglow Chocolatiers truck pulled into the parking lot.

"It's about time," Oliver muttered, perching across from her. "He's running late."

She grabbed Oliver's arm. "It can't be … Joe is in town?"

"We've had nightly conversations, and I knew he was coming this evening to see you."

Her heartbeat accelerated as a short, handsome man—carrying a package wrapped in blue paper and a thin gold bow—strode into the diner.

His usually neat flannel shirt puckered at the waist, his white hair was disheveled.

"When did you arrange this?" She squinted at him. "How?"

Oliver set the order pad on the table, a doodling of two hearts in the corner. "I'm an old-fashioned Cupid, and recommended he take action."

"Hi, Emily." Joe strode to her booth. Tears were in his eyes as he hesitantly set the box on the table. "I brought you a gift."

She stared up at him. "Joe, if it's brownies …"

"I think I'm done playing Cupid." Oliver shoved to his feet and moved to the counter. "Shall I prepare two servings of lasagna?"

Emily regarded Joe.

"Absolutely," he agreed.

Still reeling, she said stiffly, "You could have mailed the package, Joe."

"I'm not here to deliver brownies." He settled across from her, gazing at her with boyish eagerness. "I'm here to offer you what's in this box."

"Did you bake another low-calorie recipe?"

He shook his head. "Not low calorie. No calorie."

"What?" She couldn't help herself. She was staring at him.

"Please open it."

She did, and then she gasped. A polished moonstone ring, exquisite in its simple luminous beauty, was set in a magnificent gold setting.

"I wasn't sure of your ring size. However, the jewelry maker in Cambria assured me that the size can be altered."

"You bought this in Cambria?"

"I ordered it ahead, left my house before dawn and picked it up this morning. The way we parted ... it's not over. *We're* not over. I traveled halfway across the state to be with you."

"Five hours each way. That's a long drive."

"Not for the woman I love."

He loved her and was uttering the words out loud. The knowledge made her breath catch.

His voice was deep and gripping. She'd longed to hear from him, to see him.

"All this effort ... for me." She fixed her hand on top of his. He was warm, animated, dynamic.

"Our life together," he said. "There's a wonderful, exciting world waiting for us to explore."

She opened her mouth, and then closed it, celebrating the upcoming years in her mind.

He pressed his fingers to her lips. "I want to marry you, Emily, and I won't take no for an answer."

"You said you didn't want to be with me. You were

concerned about what your daughter and co-workers might assume."

"I'm ashamed of myself, because it was my own self-esteem and fears that caused the problem. I couldn't allow people to speculate that I was with you for your money. I would never use you."

"Joe, I don't care about other people's opinions."

"But I do, and I will protect you from any disparaging remarks because I love you, Emily."

"And I love you."

"Good. Good." He beamed. "I've spent many hours pondering our situation, and I figured out a workable solution."

She nodded, waiting for him to continue.

"I'll drive part time, and when I go on a trip, you'll come with me."

"But, Joe, where will we live?"

"Anywhere." He paused, then grinned. "I have nowhere to go, though, because I sold my house. However, I managed to purchase a quaint cottage in Cambria with part of my savings. It boasts an outdoor shower and is situated near the sea."

She pressed her fingers to her throat. "You bought our cottage?"

"Yep. It needs a painting, though."

"I can paint."

The infectious grin that had filled her days in Cambria settled on his features, along with a charismatic trace of conscience. "I approached the owner who was more than willing to sell for a fair price. He even threw in the two bicycles at no extra charge."

"Generous." She shared his grin at that. "What about my house?"

"Keep it, sell it. We can discuss the logistics later."

"After living there for thirty years, I'll sell." She gazed up at him with a helpless smile. "I expected to never see you again."

"Yet, here I am." He pushed up his glasses. "Will you marry me, Emily Varon?"

"Yes. Yes. Yes." For the first time, she noticed the stubble of his white beard, the strokes of weariness at the corners of his bright-blue eyes.

He secured the ring on her left hand finger, then leaned over and kissed her, gently and lovingly and expressively. She curved her hand around his nape, and he buried his kisses in her hair. From the corner of her eye, she spotted Oliver placing a cassette tape player on the counter.

"Now?" he asked Joe when they pulled back from their kiss.

Joe turned to Oliver. "Perfect."

The poignant music from Andrew Lloyd Webber's musical, *Cats,* floated through the diner. The handful of patrons looked up from their meals and smiled. Apparently, the entire diner was in on her surprise.

Emily's heart tightened. "That's my favorite song. 'Memory'."

"I found the cassette online, and I've listened to the music ever since."

"You discovered musicals," she said.

"Especially the lyrics to this song. You're not alone, Emily. Not in the moonlight, not in the daylight. We're here, together, living for today and tomorrow. We'll create our own memories."

She glimpsed Oliver opening several windows to let in a flurry of air, and then her gaze settled on Joe.

The man she loved. Their journey in unison.

"We'll create our own life events," Joe was saying.

And the beckoning of a summer breeze, lighting the landscape of their lives.

The End

A NOTE FROM JOSIE

Dear Reader,

Thank you for reading *A Chocolate-Box Summer Breeze*.

I wanted to write another story centering around the characters in the "Chocolate" series, and chose an older couple—Emily and Joe—to share a summer romance with you.

If you loved this sweet romance as much as I loved writing it, please help other people find *A Chocolate-Box Summer Breeze* by posting your review.

A Chocolate-Box Summer Breeze is available in ebook, Paperback, Large Print Paperback, Hardcover, and Audiobook.

I'd love to meet you in person someday, but in the meantime, all I can offer is a sincere and grateful thank you. Without your support, my books would not be possible.

As I write my next sweet or inspirational romance, remember this: Have you ever tried something you were afraid to try because it mattered so much to you? I did, when I started writing. Take the chance, and just do something you love.

My Spotify Play List for A Chocolate-Box Summer Breeze is here.

With sincere appreciation,

Josie Riviera

Love the "Chocolate Box" sweet romances?

Be sure to check out the other books:

Click here.

RECIPE FOR LYDIA'S PEANUT BUTTER BARS

#1 CRUST:

    1 cup margarine

    1 cup brown sugar

    ½ cup white sugar

    4 cups oatmeal

    Mix together, PRESS in an 12 x 18 ungreased pan.

    Bake 375 degrees for 12 minutes. COOL.

#2 Spread over crust.

    1 cup creamy Peanut Butter

    (Place in the garage or outside to harden.)

#3

12 – 18 ounces of chocolate chips

1 ½ - 2 Tablespoon butter

Melt together. Dot evenly over peanut butter and spread out.

#4

COOL. Cut into squares. Place into a cookie tin or a plastic container.

Refrigerate. Keeps well for up to a month.

Enjoy!

A CHOCOLATE-BOX CHRISTMAS
WISH CHAPTER ONE PREVIEW

CHAPTER ONE

High on a rain-drenched hill, Cora Carpenter set down her mug of tea and stared out the kitchen window of her bungalow. The stream of chatter from the children in her day care had ceased, leaving the quiet of a cloudy California afternoon.

She didn't focus on Evanville's town square below, which she easily spotted from her window. Soon, the square would boast hundreds of twinkling white lights as night fell. Or, if she opened her window, the faint sounds of a community concert might drift up to her.

The window remained closed, the concert quiet, because one weekly chore pervaded her thoughts. She dreaded grocery shopping on Thursdays. And today was Thursday.

Never much of a cook she found preparing a spread for a single person, namely herself, was disheartening. Not to mention it emphasized she was alone, without anyone to share meals or companionship.

She blew out a sigh. So?

So, it was no big deal, right?

Wrong.

Perhaps it was society's lofty expectations. Every television commercial promoted sharing holiday festivities with a partner.

Not her, though. She wouldn't expose herself to the hurt that inevitably followed.

She turned as Jack, her brother, breezed into the kitchen. Bald, sporting a thin black mustache, and older than she by a decade, he told everyone he was a confirmed bachelor.

"Smells good in here." He made a beeline for the cinnamon cookies on the counter. "Are you holiday baking, already?"

"Cinnamon and cream cheese are key ingredients." She gestured to the trays. "Try one."

"Only one?" He snatched a handful.

"Or take a dozen. A couple of the older children and I baked them for you and the nurses at the hospital."

"Much appreciated." He craned his neck to peer out the window. "By the way, Evanville pulled out all the stops for the holidays, complete with a strolling Christmas tree."

"I don't remember anyone mentioning a strolling tree," Cora said.

"It's an innovative idea by the town council's think tank."

"*Our* town council has a think tank?"

He winked between bites. "More like the mayor and his wife. You'll notice the tree when you visit downtown."

"How … jolly." She lifted a snowman mug to her lips and gave her reindeer earrings a toss. "What's more festive than a walking tree?"

"A *strolling* tree," he corrected. "And, there's something even more exciting."

"The live nativity?"

"The annual *candy-cane-eating contest*." Dramatically, he enunciated every word.

"A favorite of yours because you've won three years in a row." When he didn't reply, she asked, "Are you entering?"

"I probably should give other people a chance." He sported a smug grin. "But I won't. Besides, all the extra sugar in candy canes leads to only one result."

"Which is?"

He poured a mug of coffee for himself. "Obesity."

Despite herself, Cora laughed at her brother's good humor, his acceptance of himself as an overweight man. Lighthearted, embracing the comedy in life, he pushed away the loneliness in her chest.

"Are you participating in the hospital's 5K charity run?" he asked.

She smoothed her khaki-colored sweatshirt, embroidered with the likeness of a cherry-red cardinal. "Sadly, I'm out of shape."

"You're lanky and lean. Me, on the other hand ..." He patted his protruding stomach. At six feet and three hundred pounds, Jack was at a weight many people, including his doctor, labeled as morbidly obese.

"The run is important to me," he went on, "because it benefits Project Nutrition." He grabbed a napkin to wipe his mouth and tossed it in the trash. "Needless to say, I'll be walking."

"I read about the program," Cora replied. "They implement cost-effective strategies, such as adding iron to food to help cut childhood anemia."

"Malnutrition contributes to a number of developmental delays." As always, Jack spoke passionately when talking about kids. He was a nurse in the children's ward at the local hospital. Both he and Cora had chosen child-oriented occupations, and they loved youngsters, although neither of them were married nor had children.

He set down his mug and picked up a paper and pen.

"Are you taking notes on how many candy canes you're required to devour in order to win the contest?" Cora joked.

"Nope. I already know."

"How many?"

He zipped his lips with his fingers.

She chuckled at the image of a secretive Jack sitting at a table piled high with candy canes in the festively decorated town square.

"I'm an organized person and preparing my holiday shopping list," he said.

"Right now?"

"Why not?" Sheepishly, he grinned. "What's your Christmas wish this year, Cora?"

She tapped her fingers on the counter. "I can't think of anything special."

"December twenty-fifth isn't far away. You must have an idea."

"Honestly, I don't." She squinted at the paper as he quickly jotted numbers. "What are you writing?"

"My ideal weight." He presented a guilty smile and set the pen down. "And have you decided whether you'll fly to Nevada with me to visit Mom?"

"Maybe."

He let out a frustrated sigh. "That's not an answer."

Cora turned and began wrapping the cookies for him to take with him. She exhaled, only then recognizing she'd been holding her breath.

In truth, she'd made her choice. Their mother, Zoe, had raved for weeks about her latest beau, and Cora suspected that adult children would be in the way of this fresh romance. Their visit might result in an awkward situation.

Jack, apparently, harbored no such qualms.

"Well?" He counted off the days on his fingers until Christmas.

"I'll stay in town," Cora replied. "If any of my child-care parents are working extra shifts, they'll call for me to watch their kids."

"You deserve a week off."

"I want to be available just in case, but will plan to take time off between Christmas and New Year's." She provided a small smile. "We'll agree on a raincheck for me to visit Mom, okay?"

"Don't you want to accompany me on my first solo flight?"

She stiffened. "You're flying a plane yourself?"

"A commuter plane. I finally earned my pilot's license, and it's an hour flight from California to Nevada." At Cora's frown, he smiled reassuringly. "My instructor offered to fly with me."

"Olivia?" Cora's mind raced with the possibilities. "The woman with curly auburn hair down to her waist who recently graduated from college?"

"One and the same. After sixty hours of flight time, thirty of flight briefings, and forty hours of ground school, I'm ready."

"To date or to fly?"

"Both." He hooked an arm around her waist and twirled her, singing "I'll be Home For Christmas."

Laughing, she leaned against the counter to shake off the dizziness. "Are you abandoning bachelorhood for a woman fifteen years your junior?"

"Me? A man who prizes my unmarried status?" He looked out the window again and cleared his throat. "Have you spoken to Dad? I realize you might still be angry at him, what with his tendency to try to control our lives."

"*Tendency* to control?"

"Yeah, more than a tendency." Jack gave a quick laugh. "Well, have you?"

"I've reached out to him."

She chewed her bottom lip. She had no desire to revisit *that* argument. Her father's vocal opinions had left her panicked and embarrassed. In short, he'd been opposed to her dating the man she'd met online because he believed he was a con. She'd refused to listen. Her father had never liked any of the men she'd dated.

Then he'd chided her for being a silly, desperate fool, and they had quarreled. Wasn't it her decision as a grown woman to date whoever she pleased?

Besides, she wasn't desperate. Was she?

Mentally, she reviewed her childhood. Her father had always criticized her, especially after he and her mother had divorced. Don't wear revealing clothes, don't attend any university except the one he selected. His overbearing demands of how she should behave had become the thread mark of their conversations.

Now she was sorry for the argument because she'd raised her voice to her own father. He'd been right.

She swallowed the lump in her throat.

Weren't most decisions easier in hindsight?

"Don't be offended by Dad's outburst." Jack retrieved a worn teddy bear from the floor and deposited it in a plastic bin. "Refuse to let a scam artist ruin your Christmas."

She accepted Jack's words in the vein they were meant—encouragement from a caring older brother. Thankfully, he didn't press her for more details.

"So what's your wish?" he repeated.

She surveyed the kitchen—the cabinets that hadn't been painted in a decade, the leaky sink faucet, the budget-friendly linoleum.

Grimacing, she finally said, "I'd love a bright and shiny stainless-steel refrigerator."

He chuckled. "A refrigerator is not a Christmas wish."

"When it's twenty years old and formerly belonged to our parents, then it constitutes a wish." She nodded to the pen. "Write that down."

"Mom and Dad split long ago, and you can't break up with your refrigerator." He pinned her with a thoughtful gaze. "Think of something else."

"A dishwasher to replace the one I never had?"

He tapped his foot and snatched another cookie before she could to wrap it. "Nope."

"A shelving unit for baby board books?" She stepped into the living room. "Better yet, a chest full of educational toys."

"I meant a special wish for you." Jack peered at the wall clock. "My hospital shift begins at three. Keep thinking and we'll talk soon, okay?"

"Okay. I'm off to complete my least favorite task."

"Grocery shopping?"

"You know me well." She pushed a strand of hair from her face. She didn't fuss with her appearance. She'd always preferred to style her dark hair in a short pixie cut, but lately had let it grow out. Who had hours for fancy grooming while watching youngsters all day?

Jack placed his mug in the sink. "You'll stop at Olive's Diner first?"

"I'm a creature of habit." She shook her ponytail free and dug through her purse for the key to her ten-year-old Chevy. "A meal at the diner definitely brightens my Thursdays."

On the drive to town, she mulled over Jack's Christmas-wish question and chided herself on her responses. Instead of materialistic or self-centered items, she should wish for something that benefitted others.

Her mind wandered, taking inventory of her to-do list:

Home decorating, gift-giving, writing out cards, baking ...

Once, she'd treasured the Christmas holiday. The days were thrilling, not demanding. Lately, endless activities screamed to be accomplished. What did it all mean, the frantic rush to accomplish everything by New Year's? Was it acceptable to think of herself?

She switched on her car radio, and the melodic strains of "A Holly Jolly Christmas" came through the speakers. Would she ever reach a place when the holidays didn't retell what had vanished from her life?

She'd believed that Gregory Pansa loved her, and they would spend Christmas together on the beach in Florida. He'd promised. Unfortunately, he never existed.

Burl Ives continued crooning about the best time of the year, and Cora sang along. One constant hadn't changed.

Her love of music.

Thirty minutes later, Cora sat at her preferred booth in Olive's Diner, enticed by the scents of buttery mashed potatoes and a pot roast simmering with root vegetables. Comfort-foods, timeless and hearty staples.

She rotated a string of Christmas oldies in the jukebox every week while she ate.

Today was no exception, and she fed the jukebox enough coins so that Elvis Presley repeatedly belted out a tune about his blue Christmas.

Oliver, the owner and an amiable man in his thirties, stepped to the booth and poured her a cup of coffee. "How are the peanut butter cups?" he asked.

She touched her hands to her lips. "Delicious, as always. An ideal end to a wonderful meal."

"Thanks to Sally." The pride in his tone was apparent. "It's her recipe."

"Yes, so you've mentioned." *A million times.*

Oliver's hazelnut eyes lit with warmth whenever he mentioned Sally Elliot. They'd met the previous Valentine's Day when she and several other customers had been stranded at his diner because of a violent storm. She was a chocolatier and owned a candy shop in Bloomingfield, a couple hours' drive from the diner. Sally and Oliver had created the recipe that night.

"I can't make these peanut butter cups fast enough," he said. "Every Thursday, I place two aside for you."

"I admire your thoughtfulness." Cora unwrapped the second candy on her plate. "Have you and Sally planned a wedding date yet?"

"February fourteenth. Her daughter, Clarissa, will be our flower girl."

His ecstatic expression prompted Cora's smile. "Is Sally aware of your plans?"

"Not yet." A wide grin split his face. "I'm surprising her

71

with an engagement ring on Christmas day, and a Valentine wedding is—"

"Romantic." Cora clasped her hands together. The thrill of the romance brought goose bumps to her arms. "Let me add *brilliant* and *delightful*."

"I show my love on my sleeve, don't I? When it comes to Sally, I'm definitely starry-eyed."

"Don't ever change, Oliver." Despite her encouraging smile, Cora bit back a resigned sigh. When had she last experienced any of those wonderful emotions called love?

She hadn't.

That is, not until she recently met a man on an online dating platform. On a whim, she'd joined the site and uploaded her profile and picture. The man's photo displayed a middle-aged, black-bearded guy in medical scrubs by the name of Gregory Pansa.

Soon after, he'd messaged her. He was a doctor who lived in Egypt, trying desperately to return to America because he was a US citizen. Day after day he endured one obstacle after another. He was out of money because his funds were tied up in a foreign bank account, he'd been in an accident and was in the hospital. Or, the latest, he'd missed his flight to the States.

At first, she had shaken her head in exasperation. But the more he emailed, the more she believed him. Surely he wasn't scamming her, no matter what her father contended.

Not now. Not during the holidays.

Gregory complimented her "soulful amber eyes rimmed by generous black lashes" and her "velvety-smooth complexion." She embraced his poetic words since they brought a rush of exhilaration. Perhaps Gregory was *the one.*

Her father investigated further, drawing her attention to numerous inconsistencies with Gregory's story. Finally, she faced the fact that Gregory Pansa wasn't real.

She'd been a fool. Plus, she was out two thousand dollars.

She sank back in the booth and allowed Elvis Presley's deep voice to carry a note of warmth into a chilly afternoon.

The diner's door swung open and a tall man filled the entrance with his broad shoulders and strong frame. His handsome, sun-kissed face set in a mild frown while he surveyed the diner. Quickly, he strode to the counter as Oliver emerged from the kitchen carrying a tray of red velvet cakes.

Cora turned to watch their exchange. Customer chats around her table stilted.

"Is there a garage nearby?" the man inquired. "My car broke down a mile from here."

Oliver set down the tray. "Were you in a car wreck? Are you all right?"

"No. I'm fine."

"You walked?"

"It isn't far."

"Far enough. Fortunately, the rain never started."

"Right." Grimly, the man looked toward the window, then at Oliver. "Are you the cook?"

Oliver gave a slight bow. "I'm the owner. Oliver."

"Patrick Gervez." The man removed his black leather gloves, shoved them into the pockets of his tan wool coat, and the men shook hands. "I'm on my way to Bloomingfield."

*** End of Excerpt A Chocolate-Box Christmas Wish by Josie Riviera ***

Copyright © 2020 Josie Riviera

Want more? Keep reading A Chocolate-Box Christmas Wish.

Available on Amazon! FREE on Kindle Unlmited

Love the Chocolate-Box Series? Grab all the books here:

Or grab Chocolate-Box Double Hearts here.
All six "Chocolate-Box" books in 1 sweet bundle.

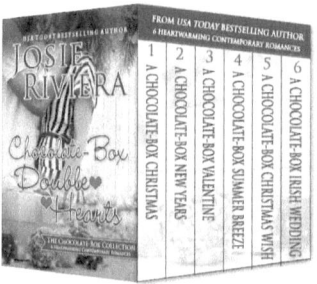

ABOUT THE AUTHOR

Josie Riviera is a *USA TODAY* bestselling author of contemporary, inspirational, and historical sweet romances that read like Hallmark movies. She lives in the Charlotte, NC, area with her wonderfully supportive husband. They share their home with an adorable shih tzu, who constantly needs grooming, and live in an old house forever needing renovations.

To receive my Newsletter and your free sweet romance novella ebook as a thank you gift, sign up HERE.

Become a member of my Read and Review VIP Facebook group for exclusive giveaways and ARCs.

josieriviera.com/

ACKNOWLEDGMENTS

An appreciative thank you to my patient husband, Dave, and our three wonderful children.

Cherished Hearts Six Book Volume

Aloha To Love

Sweet Peppermint Kisses

Valentine Hearts Boxed Set

1-800-CUPID

1-800-CHRISTMAS

1-800-IRELAND

1-800-SUMMER

1-800-NEW YEAR

Irish Hearts Sweet Romance Bundle

Holly's Gift

A Chocolate-Box Christmas

A Chocolate-Box New Years

A Chocolate-Box Valentine

A Chocolate-Box Summer Breeze

A Chocolate-Box Christmas Wish

A Chocolate-Box Irish Wedding

Chocolate-Box Hearts

Chocolate-Box Hearts Volume Two

Chocolate-Box Double Hearts

Recipes From The Heart

Leading Hearts

New Year Hearts

SENIOR HEARTS

Summer Hearts

Christmas in the Air (1-800-Book)

A Very Christian Christmas

The 1-800-Series Volume Two

The 1-800-Series Complete

Christmas Tails of the Heart

Cocoa's Christmas Love

Pawfect Christmas Hearts

Pink Coral Island

Most books are available in ebook, audiobook, paperback, Large Print paperback and Hardcover.

Many are FREE on Kindle Unlimited!

www.ingramcontent.com/pod-product-compliance
Lightning Source LLC
Chambersburg PA
CBHW031209260626

47169CB00004B/1300

*9 7 8 1 9 5 1 9 5 1 0 8 5 *